HOLBERG SUITE
and Other Orchestral Works
in Full Score

Edvard Grieg

DOVER PUBLICATIONS, INC.
Mineola, New York

Bibliographical Note

This Dover edition, first published in 2001, is a new compilation of six works originally published separately by C. F. Peters, Leipzig, n.d., including *Zwei elegische Melodien,* Op. 34; *Aus Holberg's Zeit,* Op. 40; *Altnorwegische Romanze mit Variationen,* Op. 51; *Zwei Melodien,* Op. 53; *Lyrische Suite,* from Opus 54; and *Zwei lyrische Stücke,* from Opus 68.

Lists of annotated contents and instrumentation, as well as main headings in the music, are newly added. German score notes and footnotes have been translated into English.

We are grateful to The Sibley Music Library, Eastman School of Music, for their gracious loan of these rare scores for republication.

International Standard Book Number: 0-486-41692-5

Manufactured in the United States of America
Dover Publications, Inc., 31 East 2nd Street, Mineola, N.Y. 11501

CONTENTS

INSTRUMENTATION

Two Elegiac Melodies, Op. 34 (p. 1)
    String orchestra

From Holberg's Time: Suite in Olden Style, Op. 40 (p. 6)
    String orchestra

Old Norwegian Romance with Variations, Op. 51 (p. 23)
    3 Flutes (dbl. piccolo), 2 oboes, 2 clarinets, 2 bassoons
    4 horns, 2 trumpets, 3 trombones, tuba
    timpani, percussion, harp, strings

Two Melodies, Op. 53 (p. 107)
    String orchestra

Lyric Suite, Op. 54

    "Shepherd boy" (p. 116)
    Harp and strings

    "Norwegian rustic march" (p. 123)
    2 Flutes, 2 oboes, 2 clarinets, 2 bassoons
    4 horns, 2 trumpets, 3 trombones, tuba
    timpani, harp, strings

    "Notturno" (p. 136)
    Piccolo, 2 flutes, 2 oboes, 2 clarinets, 2 bassoons
    4 horns, timpani, triangle, harp, strings

    "March of the trolls" (p. 149)
    Piccolo, 2 flutes, 2 oboes, 2 clarinets, 2 bassoons
    4 horns, 2 trumpets, 3 trombones, tuba
    timpani, bass drum & cymbals
    harp, strings

Two Lyric Pieces, from Op. 68

    "Evening in the mountains" (p. 172)
    Oboe, horn, strings

    "Cradle song" (p. 176)
    String orchestra

HOLBERG SUITE

and Other Orchestral Works
in Full Score

Two Elegiac Melodies
Op. 34

The wounded heart • *Hjertesår*

Composer's 1881 string orchestra transcription of the song Op. 33, No. 3 (1880) (poem by A. O. Vinje)

Spring • *Våren*

Composer's 1881 string orchestra transcription of the song Op. 33, No. 2 (1880) (poem by A. O. Vinje)

From Holberg's Time
Suite in Olden Style, Op. 40

Composer's orchestration for strings of the work composed for solo piano (both, 1884)

Praeludium

Ludwig Holberg (1684–1754), the "Molière of the North," is the creator of modern Danish–Norwegian literature.

II Sarabande

*) Lift bow **) Change of bowing

Gavotte

MUSETTE.

Poco più mosso.

Air

Rigaudon

Allegro con brio. ♩ = 144.

From Holberg's Time / 21

Old Norwegian Romance
with Variations

Op. 51

Composer's 1900 orchestration of the work composed for two pianos (1891)

23

Finale.

Allegro molto marcato. ♩ = 100.

Two Melodies
Op. 53

Norwegian • *Norsk*

Composer's 1891 string orchestra transcription of the song *Fyremål* *(The goal)*, Op. 33, No. 12 (1880)
(poem by A. O. Vinje)

The first meeting • *Det første møde*

Composer's 1891 string orchestra transcription of the song Op. 21, No. 1 (1870)
(poem by Björnsterne Björnson)

Lyric Suite
Op. 54

Composer's 1904 orchestration of Nos. 1, 2, 4 and 3 from six *Lyric Pieces*, Op. 54, for solo piano (1891)

Shepherd boy • *Gjaetergut*

*) This measure, as well as later measures with similar content, are to be performed *rubato*; specifically, the first few notes should always be held back a bit, and the following notes accelerated more and more.

Norwegian rustic march • *Gangar*

Notturno

*) Execution:

March of the trolls • *Troldtog*

NB: All notes marked + are stopped.

Two Lyric Pieces
from Op. 68

Evening in the mountains • *Aften på höjfjeldet*

Composer's 1898 orchestration of No. 4 from six *Lyric Pieces,* Op. 68, for solo piano (1898)

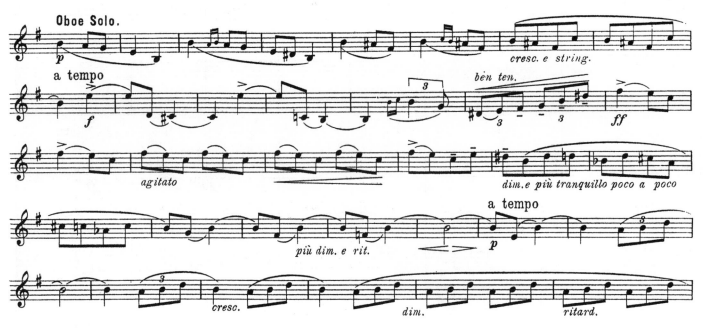

NB. ★ = Stopped note

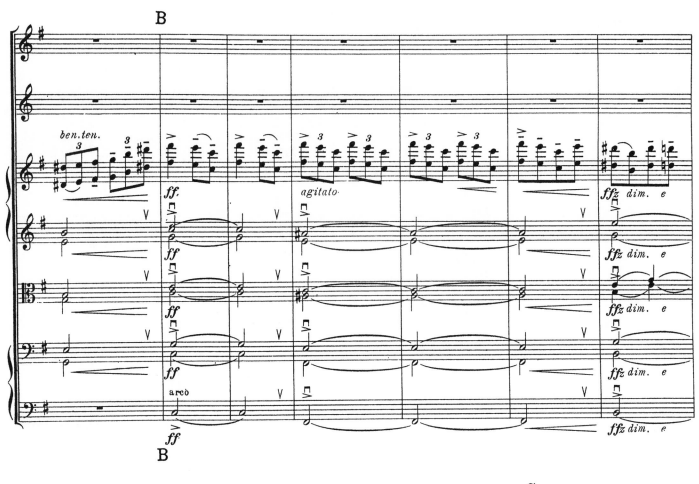

Cradle song • *Bådnlåt*

Composer's 1898 orchestration of No. 5 from six *Lyric Pieces*, Op. 68, for solo piano (1898)

Allegretto con moto.